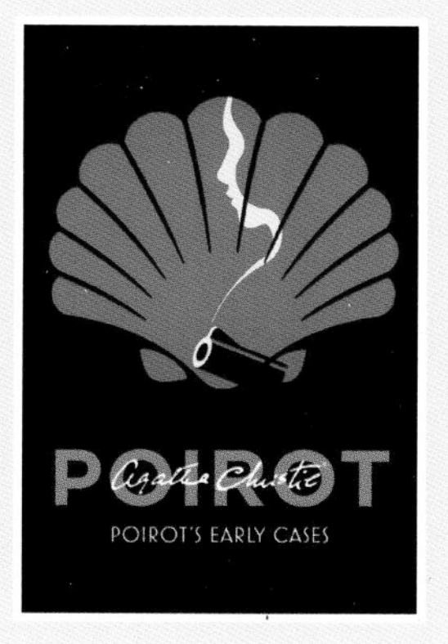

POIROT'S EARLY CASES

Aristocrats, royalty and millionaires, beautiful actresses and disappearing cooks, family curses and precious jewels, sleights of hand, poisonings and kidnappings, thieves, fraudsters, cheats and murderers. In stories harking back to the earlier years of his career, this superlative collection of tales from the Queen of Crime shows Hercule Poirot applying his famous 'little grey cells' to ever more impossible problems.

HERCULE POIROT

Over a century ago, a diminutive Belgian detective with a distinctive egg-shaped head made his first unforgettable appearance in print. With her debut novel, 1920's *The Mysterious Affair at Styles*, Agatha Christie simultaneously launched herself as a literary name and introduced readers to one of the most indelible characters ever created: Monsieur Hercule Poirot. He went on to appear in thirty-three novels and over fifty short stories, becoming Christie's most famous and long-running character and changing crime fiction for ever more. In fact, such is his fame that he remains the only fictional character to have merited a *New York Times* obituary.

Somehow this 'quaint, dandified little man', a foreigner with meticulous ways and an elaborate moustache, with his unsurpassed intelligence and unique insight into human frailty, understood the British better than they did themselves. Rapidly ensconcing himself at the very pinnacle of the establishment as high society's foremost private investigator, he repeatedly astounded both fellow characters and the reading public alike with the deployment of his famous little grey cells. Over and over, Hercule Poirot proved himself to be, without doubt, the world's greatest detective.

AGATHA CHRISTIE

Agatha Christie was born in Torquay in 1890 and became, quite simply, the bestselling novelist in history. Her first novel, *The Mysterious Affair at Styles*, written towards the end of the First World War, introduced us to Hercule Poirot, who was to become the most popular detective in crime fiction since Sherlock Holmes, with Miss Jane Marple following in 1927. She is known throughout the world as the Queen of Crime, and her books have sold over a billion copies in the English language and another billion in foreign languages. Christie is the author of sixty-six crime novels, over one hundred and fifty short stories, twenty-four plays, two autobiographical works, and six novels under the name of Mary Westmacott, and saw her work translated into more languages than Shakespeare. Her enduring success, enhanced by many film and TV adaptations, is a tribute to the timeless appeal of her characters and the unequalled ingenuity of the plots.

THE BIG FOUR

POIROT
THE BIG FOUR

Framed in the doorway of Poirot's bedroom stood a man coated from head to foot in dust. The intruder's gaunt face stared for a moment, then he swayed and fell. Who was he? Was he suffering from shock or just exhaustion? Above all, what was the significance of the figure 4, scribbled over and over again on a sheet of paper? Hercule Poirot finds himself plunged into a world of international intrigue, risking his life to uncover the truth about 'Number Four'.

JANUARY

MONDAY	TUESDAY	WEDNESDAY	THURSDAY	FRIDAY	SATURDAY	SUNDAY
		1 New Year's Day	2 Bank Holiday (Scotland)	3	4	5
6 ◐ First Quarter	7	8	9	10	11	12
13 ○ Full Moon	14	15	16	17	18	19
20	21 ◑ Third Quarter	22	23	24	25	26
27	28	29 ● Chinese New Year; New Moon	30	31		

THE MYSTERY OF THE BLUE TRAIN

On arrival in Nice, a passenger on board the luxurious sleeper, *Le Train Bleu*, is found murdered. The wealthy young woman, estranged from her husband and en route to her lover, has been strangled. And the 'Heart of Fire', the famous ruby that was in her possession, is missing. Poirot is convinced not all is as it seems – who is who they claim to be, and who, perhaps, is not?

FEBRUARY

MONDAY	TUESDAY	WEDNESDAY	THURSDAY	FRIDAY	SATURDAY	SUNDAY
					1	2
3 St Brigid's Day Holiday (ROI)	4	5 ◐	6	7	8	9
10	11	12 ○	13	14 St Valentine's Day	15	16
17	18	19	20 ◑	21	22	23
24	25	26	27	28 ● Ramadan begins		

POIROT INVESTIGATES

First there was the mystery of the film star and the diamond, then came the 'suicide' that was a murder, the mystery of the absurdly cheap flat, and a suspicious death in a locked gun-room. What links these fascinating cases and many more in this, the Queen of Crime's very first collection of stories? Only the brilliant deductive powers of Hercule Poirot!

MARCH

MONDAY	TUESDAY	WEDNESDAY	THURSDAY	FRIDAY	SATURDAY	SUNDAY
					1 St David's Day (Wales)	2
3	4 Shrove Tuesday	5 Ash Wednesday	6 ◐	7	8	9
10 Commonwealth Day	11	12	13	14 ○	15	16
17 St Patrick's Day (NI & ROI)	18	19	20 Vernal Equinox	21	22 ◑	23
24 / 31	25	26	27	28	29 ●	30 Mothering Sunday; Summer Time begins; Ramadan ends; Eid al Fitr

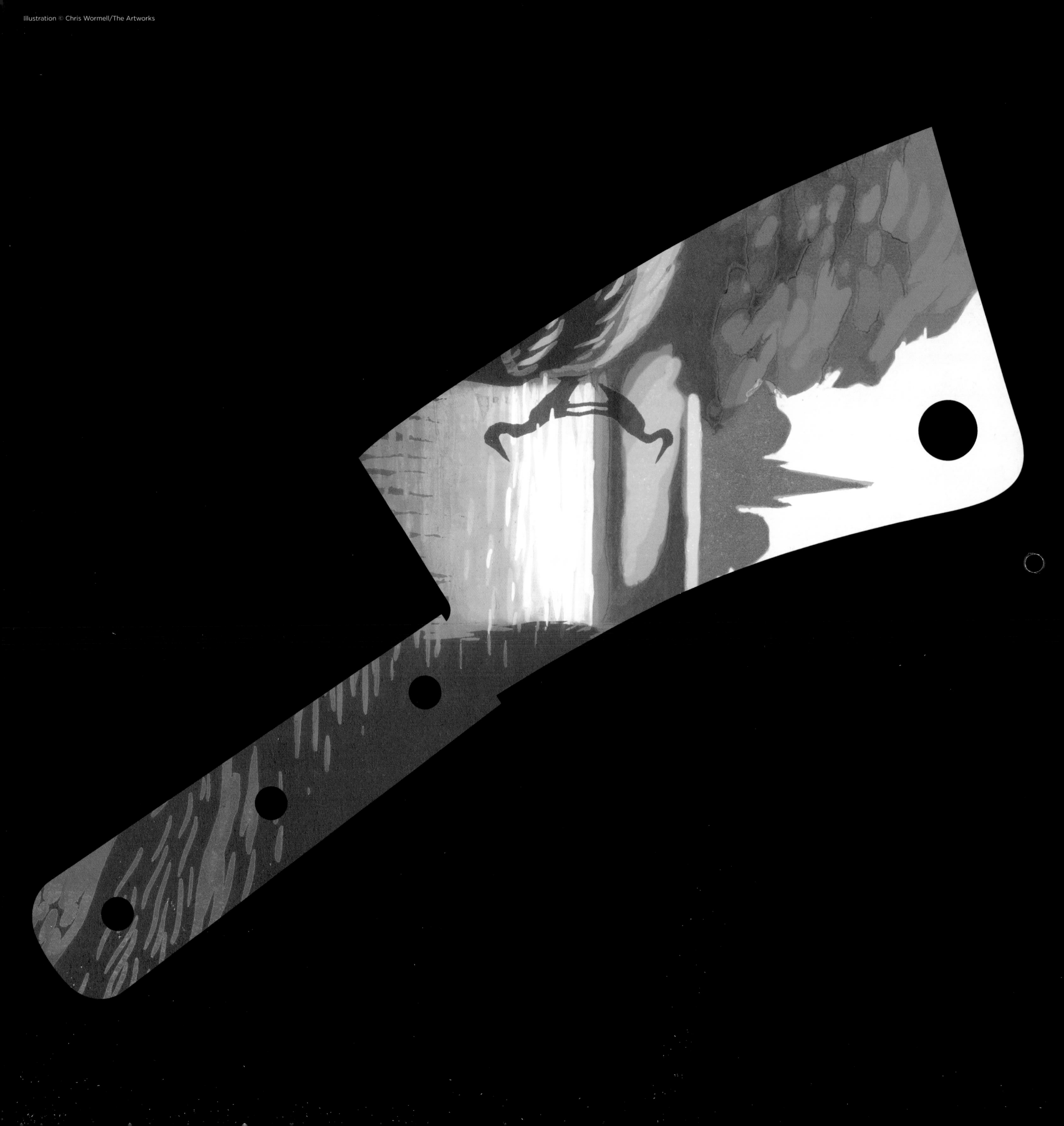

MRS MCGINTY'S DEAD

Mrs McGinty was killed by a crushing blow to the back of the head and her pitifully small savings were stolen. Could the answer lie in an article the deceased clipped from a newspaper two days before her death? Suspicion falls immediately on her lodger, hard up and out of a job. Hercule Poirot has other ideas. With a desperate killer still free, Poirot will have to stay alive long enough to find out . . .

APRIL

MONDAY	TUESDAY	WEDNESDAY	THURSDAY	FRIDAY	SATURDAY	SUNDAY
	1	2	3	4	5 ◐	6
7	8	9	10	11	12 First day of Passover	13 ○ Palm Sunday
14	15	16	17	18 Good Friday	19	20 Easter Sunday; Last day of Passover
21 ◑ Easter Monday	22	23 St George's Day (England)	24	25	26	27 ●
28	29	30				

CAT AMONG THE PIGEONS

Late one night, two teachers investigate a mysterious flashing light while the rest of the school sleeps. In the sports pavilion, among the lacrosse sticks, they stumble upon the body of the unpopular games mistress – shot through the heart from point-blank range. The school is thrown into chaos when the 'cat' strikes again. Unfortunately, schoolgirl Julia Upjohn knows too much. In particular, she knows that without Hercule Poirot's help, she will be the next victim . . .

MAY

MONDAY	TUESDAY	WEDNESDAY	THURSDAY	FRIDAY	SATURDAY	SUNDAY
			1	2	3	4 ◐
5 Early May Bank Holiday	6	7	8	9	10	11
12 ○	13	14	15	16	17	18
19	20 ◑	21	22	23	24	25
26 Spring Bank Holiday	27 ●	28	29	30	31	

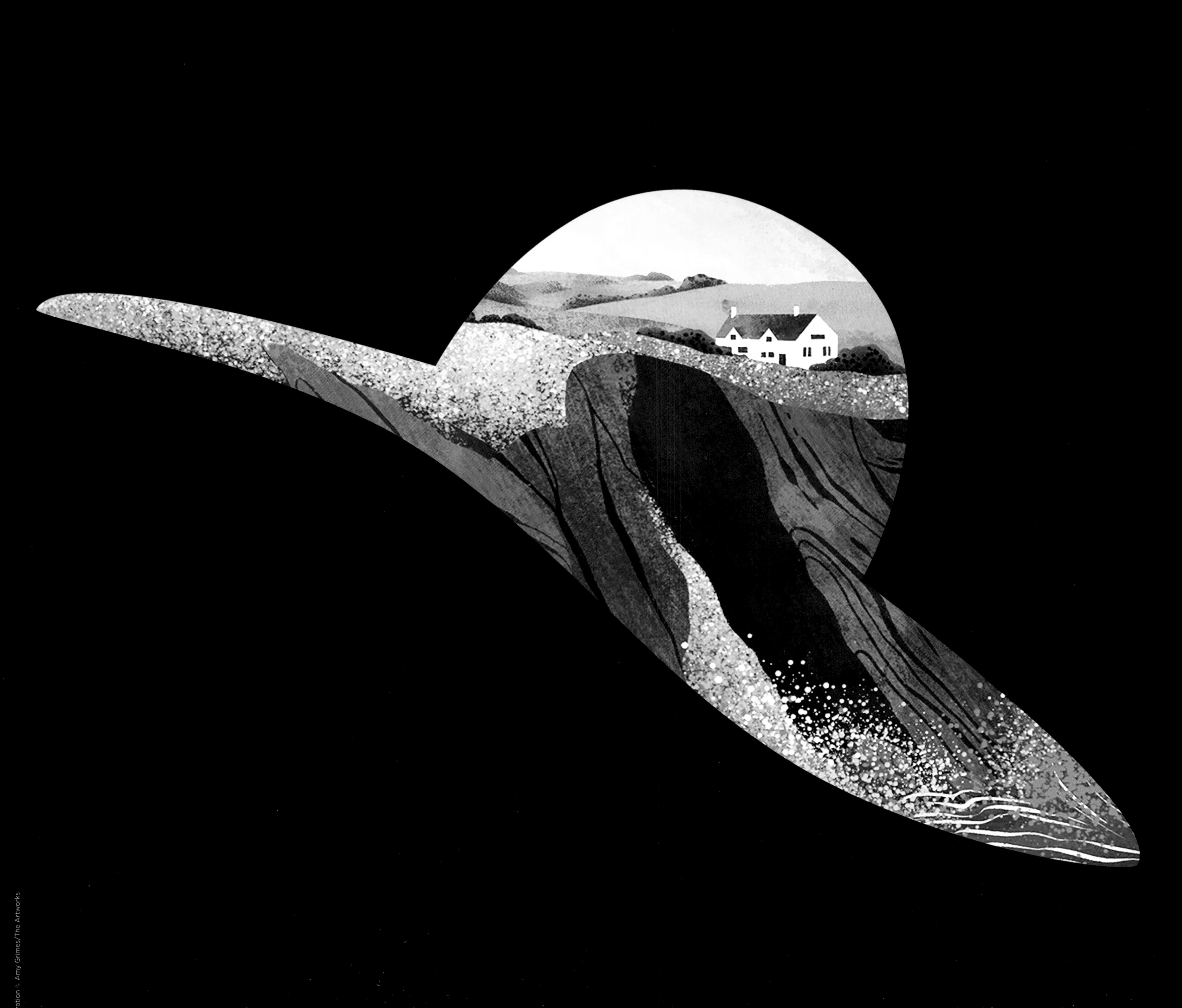

PERIL AT END HOUSE

On holiday in Cornwall, Poirot meets a pretty young woman with an unusual name, 'Nick' Buckley. Upon discovering a bullet-hole in Nick's sun hat, the great detective decides the girl needs his protection. He also begins to unravel the mystery of a murder that hasn't been committed. Yet.

JUNE

MONDAY	TUESDAY	WEDNESDAY	THURSDAY	FRIDAY	SATURDAY	SUNDAY
						1
2 Bank Holiday (ROI)	3 ◐	4	5	6 Eid-ul-Adha	7	8 Whit Sunday
9	10	11 ○	12	13	14	15 Father's Day
16	17	18 ◑	19	20	21 Summer Solstice	22
23 / 30	24	25 ● Islamic New Year	26	27	28	29

Illustration: Shutterstock.com

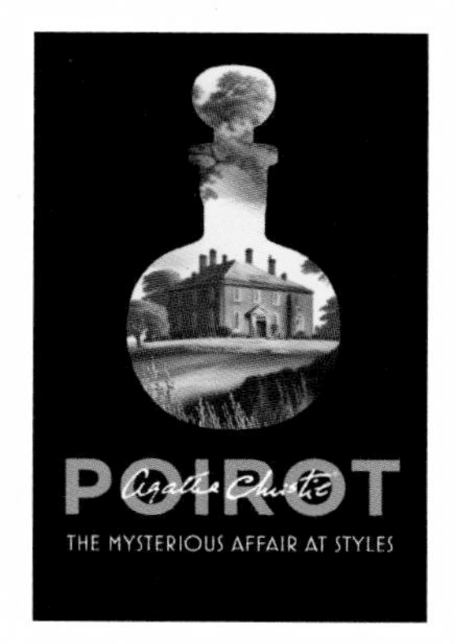

THE MYSTERIOUS AFFAIR AT STYLES

After the Great War, life can never be the same again. Captain Arthur Hastings is invited to Styles to recuperate from injuries sustained at the Front. It is the last place he expects to encounter murder. Fortunately he knows a former detective, a Belgian refugee, who happens to be staying nearby . . . Here, for the first time, meet Agatha Christie's legendary creation: Hercule Poirot.

JULY

MONDAY	TUESDAY	WEDNESDAY	THURSDAY	FRIDAY	SATURDAY	SUNDAY
	1	2 ◐	3	4	5	6
7	8	9	10 ○	11	12	13
14 Holiday (NI)	15	16	17	18 ◑	19	20
21	22	23	24 ●	25	26	27
28	29	30	31			

DEAD MAN'S FOLLY

While organising a mock murder hunt for the village fête, a feeling of dread settles on the famous crime novelist Ariadne Oliver. Call it instinct, but it's a feeling she just can't explain . . . or get away from. In desperation she summons her old friend, Hercule Poirot – and her instincts are soon proved correct when the 'pretend' murder victim is discovered playing the scene for real, a rope wrapped tightly around her neck. Under the surface of the supposedly harmless game, everyone is playing a part . . .

AUGUST

MONDAY	TUESDAY	WEDNESDAY	THURSDAY	FRIDAY	SATURDAY	SUNDAY
				1 ◐	2	3
4 Summer Bank Holiday (Scotland & ROI)	5	6	7	8	9 ○	10
11	12	13	14	15	16 ◑	17
18	19	20	21	22	23 ●	24
25 Summer Bank Holiday	26	27	28	29	30	31 ◐

THE HOLLOW

Lucy Angkatell had invited Hercule Poirot to lunch. To tease the great detective, her guests stage a mock murder beside the swimming pool. Unfortunately, the victim plays the scene for real. As his blood drips into the water, John Christow gasps one final word: 'Henrietta'. In the confusion, a gun sinks to the bottom of the pool. Poirot's enquiries reveal a complex web of romantic attachments: everyone is a suspect – and each a victim of love.

SEPTEMBER

MONDAY	TUESDAY	WEDNESDAY	THURSDAY	FRIDAY	**SATURDAY**	**SUNDAY**
1	2	3	4	5	6	7 ○
8	9	10	11	12	13	14 ◑
15 Agatha Christie born, 1890	16	17	18	19	20	21 ●
22 Autumnal Equinox; Rosh Hashanah begins	23	24 Rosh Hashanah ends	25	26	27	28
29	30 ◐					

THIRD GIRL

Three young women share a London flat. One is a coolly efficient personal secretary; another is an artist. The third, meanwhile, interrupts Hercule Poirot's breakfast of brioche and chocolat insisting that she is a murderer – and then promptly disappears. Slowly, Poirot learns of the rumours surrounding the mysterious third girl, her family – and her disappearance. Yet hard evidence is needed before the great detective can pronounce her guilty, innocent or insane . . .

OCTOBER

MONDAY	TUESDAY	WEDNESDAY	THURSDAY	FRIDAY	SATURDAY	SUNDAY
		1 Yom Kippur begins	2	3	4	5
6	7 ○	8	9	10	11	12
13 ◑	14	15	16	17	18	19
20 Diwali	21 ●	22	23	24 United Nations Day	25	26 Summer Time ends
27 Bank Holiday (ROI)	28	29 ◐	30	31 Hallowe'en		

Illustration © James Weston Lewis/The Artworks

TAKEN AT THE FLOOD

A few weeks after marrying an attractive young widow, Gordon Cloade is tragically killed by a bomb blast in the London Blitz. Overnight, the former Mrs Underhay finds herself in sole possession of the Cloade family fortune. Shortly afterwards, Hercule Poirot receives a visit from the dead man's sister-in-law, who claims she has been warned by 'spirits' that Mrs Underhay's first husband is still alive. Poirot, understandably, has his own suspicions . . .

NOVEMBER

MONDAY	TUESDAY	WEDNESDAY	THURSDAY	FRIDAY	**SATURDAY**	**SUNDAY**
					1	2
3	4	5 ○	6	7	8	9 Remembrance Sunday
10	11	12 ◑	13	14	15	16
17	18	19	20 ●	21	22	23
24	25	26	27	28 ◐	29	30 St Andrew's Day (Scotland)

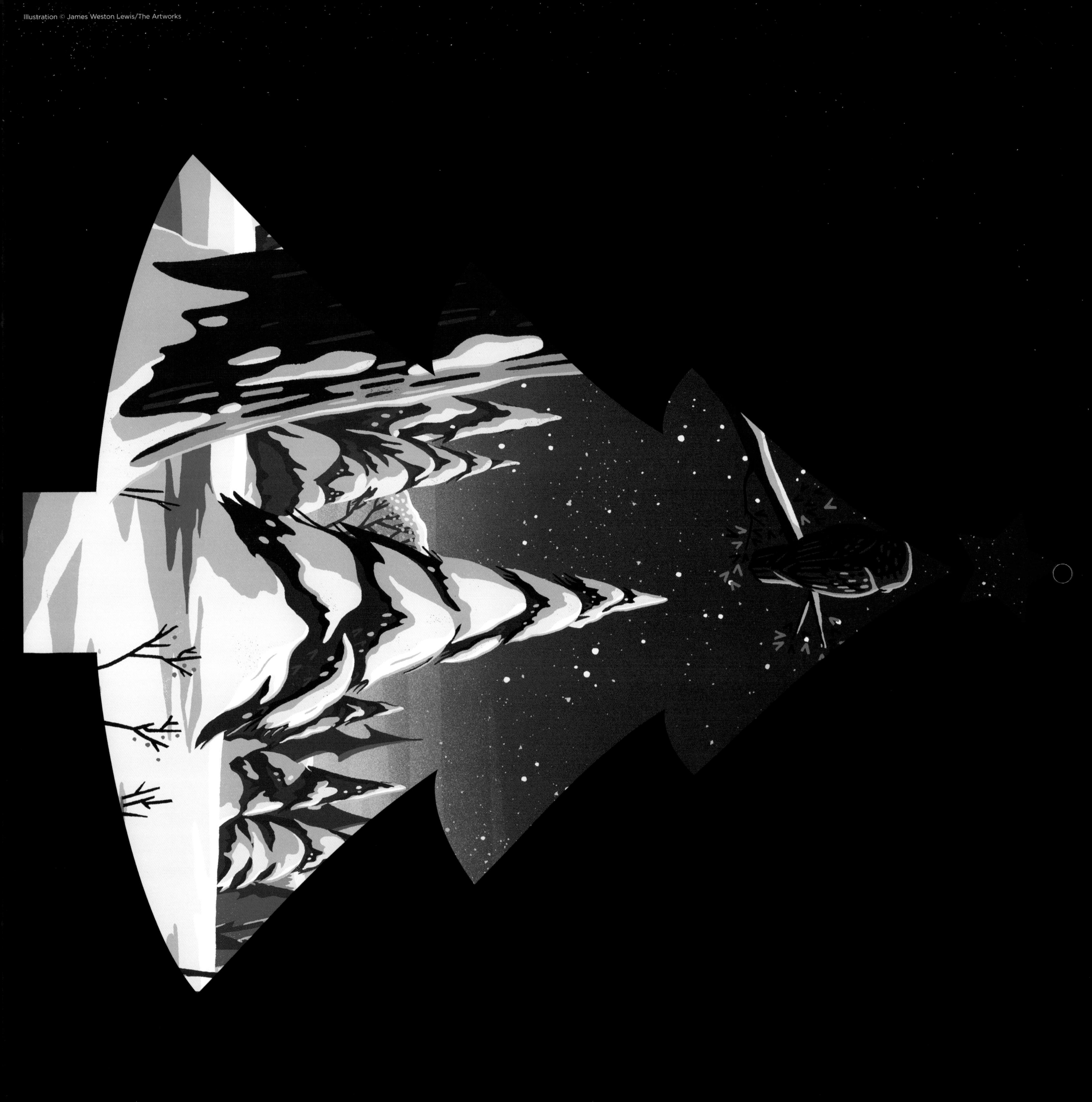

THE ADVENTURE OF THE CHRISTMAS PUDDING

The world's greatest detective always plays his cards close to his chest – until the discovery of a young woman lying in the snow spurs Poirot into revealing his hand. Six uniquely baffling cases to delight the reader, in which Hercule Poirot and also Miss Jane Marple both prove that their powers of detection are unsurpassed.

DECEMBER

MONDAY	TUESDAY	WEDNESDAY	THURSDAY	FRIDAY	SATURDAY	SUNDAY
1 Bank Holiday (Scotland)	2	3	4 ○	5	6	7
8	9	10	11 ◑	12	13	14
15	16	17	18	19	20 ●	21 Winter Solstice
22	23	24	25 Christmas Day; Hanukkah begins	26 Boxing Day; St Stephen's Day (ROI)	27 ◐	28
29	30	31 New Year's Eve				

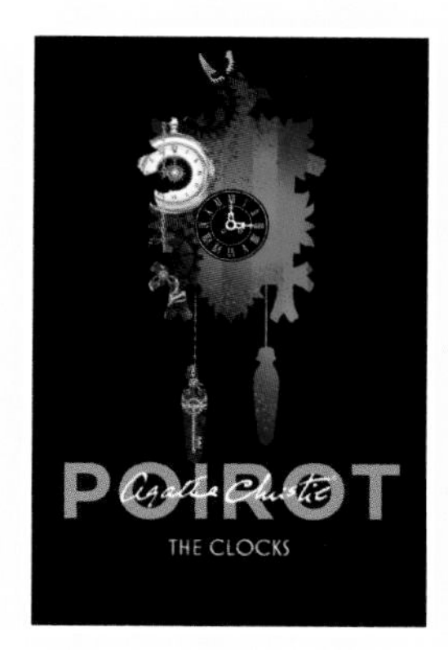

THE CLOCKS

When the Cavendish Bureau was asked to send one of their secretaries to a house in Wilbraham Crescent, the caller made no mention of the dead body she would find there. Who made the call to the agency? Who was the murdered man? And why were there clocks in the room that didn't belong there? The clocks had stopped, but the time is ticking away for Hercule Poirot . . .

2026

JANUARY

M	T	W	T	F	S	S
			1	2	3	4
5	6	7	8	9	10	11
12	13	14	15	16	17	18
19	20	21	22	23	24	25
26	27	28	29	30	31	

FEBRUARY

M	T	W	T	F	S	S
						1
2	3	4	5	6	7	8
9	10	11	12	13	14	15
16	17	18	19	20	21	22
23	24	25	26	27	28	

MARCH

M	T	W	T	F	S	S
						1
2	3	4	5	6	7	8
9	10	11	12	13	14	15
16	17	18	19	20	21	22
23	24	25	26	27	28	29
30	31					

APRIL

M	T	W	T	F	S	S
		1	2	3	4	5
6	7	8	9	10	11	12
13	14	15	16	17	18	19
20	21	22	23	24	25	26
27	28	29	30			

MAY

M	T	W	T	F	S	S
				1	2	3
4	5	6	7	8	9	10
11	12	13	14	15	16	17
18	19	20	21	22	23	24
25	26	27	28	29	30	31

JUNE

M	T	W	T	F	S	S
1	2	3	4	5	6	7
8	9	10	11	12	13	14
15	16	17	18	19	20	21
22	23	24	25	26	27	28
29	30					

JULY

M	T	W	T	F	S	S
		1	2	3	4	5
6	7	8	9	10	11	12
13	14	15	16	17	18	19
20	21	22	23	24	25	26
27	28	29	30	31		

AUGUST

M	T	W	T	F	S	S
					1	2
3	4	5	6	7	8	9
10	11	12	13	14	15	16
17	18	19	20	21	22	23
24	25	26	27	28	29	30
31						

SEPTEMBER

M	T	W	T	F	S	S
	1	2	3	4	5	6
7	8	9	10	11	12	13
14	15	16	17	18	19	20
21	22	23	24	25	26	27
28	29	30				

OCTOBER

M	T	W	T	F	S	S
			1	2	3	4
5	6	7	8	9	10	11
12	13	14	15	16	17	18
19	20	21	22	23	24	25
26	27	28	29	30	31	

NOVEMBER

M	T	W	T	F	S	S
						1
2	3	4	5	6	7	8
9	10	11	12	13	14	15
16	17	18	19	20	21	22
23	24	25	26	27	28	29
30						

DECEMBER

M	T	W	T	F	S	S
	1	2	3	4	5	6
7	8	9	10	11	12	13
14	15	16	17	18	19	20
21	22	23	24	25	26	27
28	29	30	31			

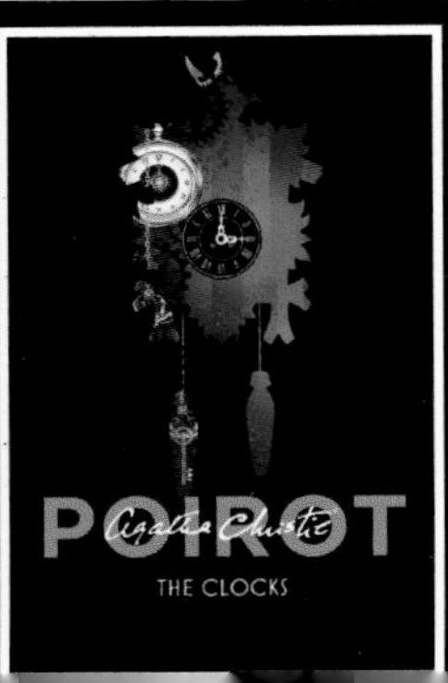

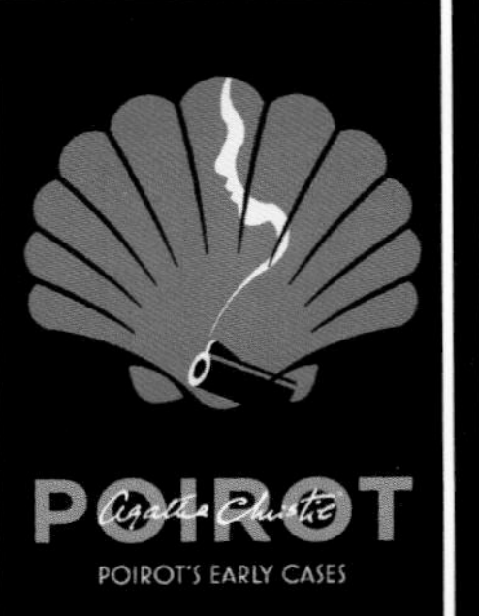

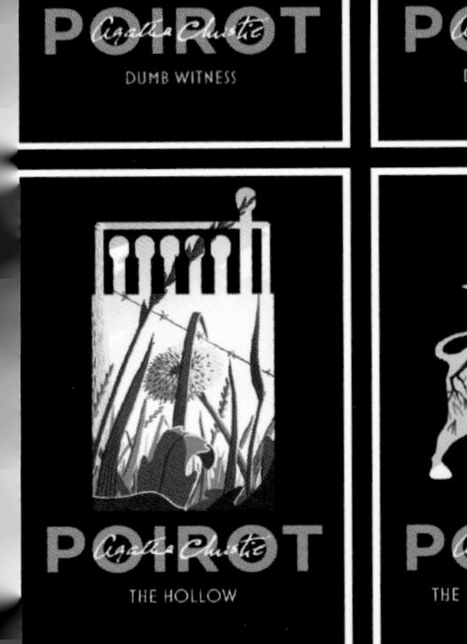

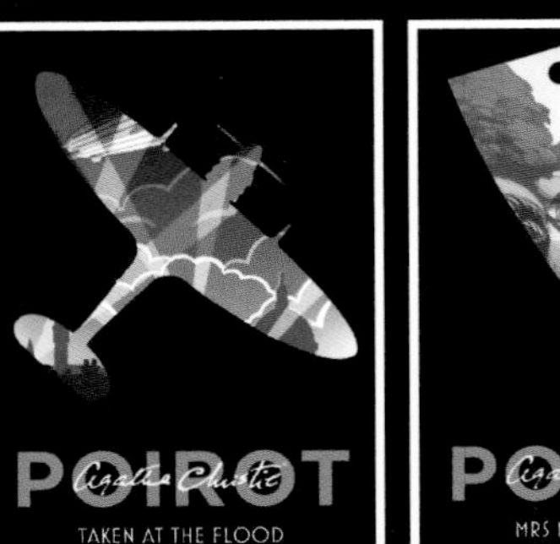
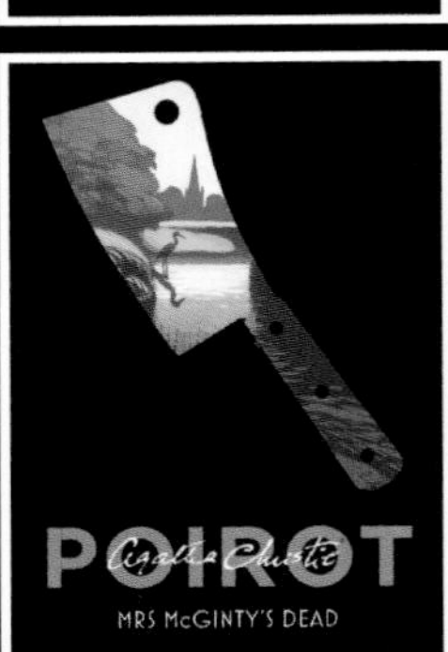
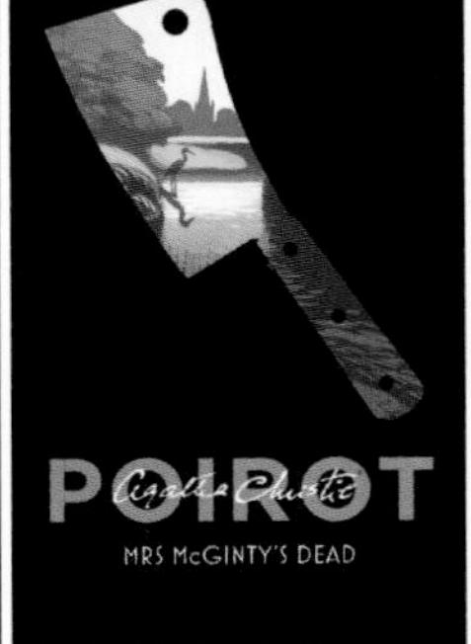
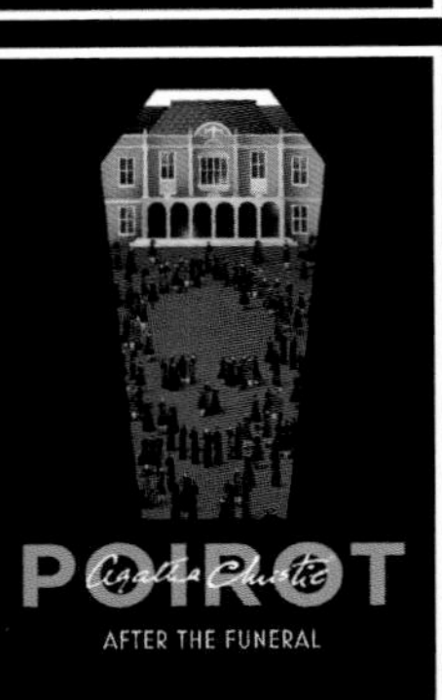
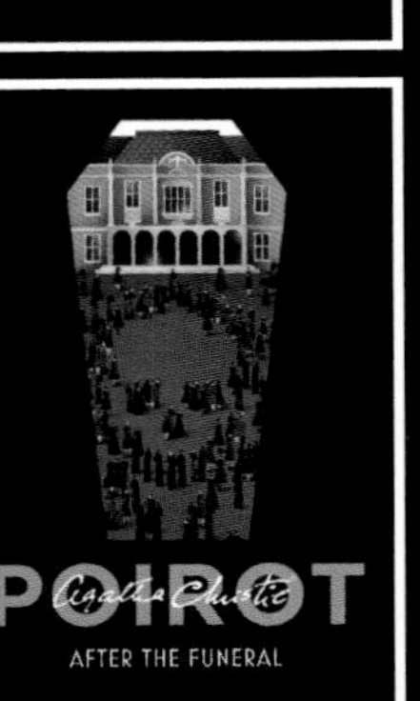

POIROT
THE MYSTERIOUS AFFAIR AT STYLES
THE MURDER ON THE LINKS
POIROT INVESTIGATES
THE MURDER OF ROGER ACKROYD
THE BIG FOUR
THE MYSTERY OF THE BLUE TRAIN
BLACK COFFEE
PERIL AT END HOUSE
LORD EDGWARE DIES
MURDER ON THE ORIENT EXPRESS
THREE ACT TRAGEDY
DEATH IN THE CLOUDS
THE ABC MURDERS
MURDER IN MESOPOTAMIA
CARDS ON THE TABLE
MURDER IN THE MEWS
DUMB WITNESS
DEATH ON THE NILE
APPOINTMENT WITH DEATH
HERCULE POIROT'S CHRISTMAS
SAD CYPRESS
ONE, TWO, BUCKLE MY SHOE
EVIL UNDER THE SUN
FIVE LITTLE PIGS
THE HOLLOW
THE LABOURS OF HERCULES
TAKEN AT THE FLOOD
MRS McGINTY'S DEAD
AFTER THE FUNERAL
HICKORY DICKORY DOCK
DEAD MAN'S FOLLY
CAT AMONG THE PIGEONS
THE ADVENTURE OF THE CHRISTMAS PUDDING
THE CLOCKS
THIRD GIRL
HALLOWE'EN PARTY
ELEPHANTS CAN REMEMBER
POIROT'S EARLY CASES
CURTAIN: POIROT'S LAST CASE
'What a magnificent book! I couldn't put it down.' SOPHIE HANNAH
Agatha Christie
POIROT
THE GREATEST DETECTIVE IN THE WORLD
MARK ALDRIDGE
FOREWORD BY MARK GATISS